RICHARD SCARRY

The Night Before the Night Before Christmas!

First published in Great Britain in 1999
This edition published by HarperCollins Children's Books in 2005
HarperCollins Children's Books is a division of HarperCollins Publishers Ltd.

1 3 5 7 9 10 8 6 4 2
0-00-720721-2

Printed and bound in China

RICHARD SCARRY

The Night Before the Night Before Christmas!

HarperCollins *Children's Books*

'Twas the night before the night before the night before Christmas, and all through the Cat family house, not a creature was stirring...
... almost.

Sally Cat can't sleep.

"Huckle?" Sally asks. "When is Santa coming?
I can't wait any longer for Christmas!"
"Just a few more days, Sally," Huckle says.
"Now go back to sleep. Good night!"

Christmas Spirit

"Oh, my!" says Mr. Frumble. "It's almost Christmas!" Mr. Frumble loves Christmas, because then he can help others in true Christmas Spirit.

He holds the door open at the grocery store. But that doesn't make Grocer Hank very happy.

Mr. Frumble offers to shovel snow, but that doesn't make Father Cat very happy.

Mr. Frumble offers to carry Hilda Hippo's Christmas gifts.

He helps Mr. Gronkle place his Christmas tree on his car.

But he makes no one happy.
"Hmm," thinks Mr. Frumble, "if no one in
Busytown needs my help before Christmas,
I think I know someone else who does!"

Mr. Frumble gets into his pickle car,
and drives over to Mr. Fixit's workshop.

Does Mr. Fixit need Mr. Frumble's help? Of course, not!
Mr. Frumble needs Mr. Fixit's help!

Mr. Frumble explains to Mr. Fixit what he needs.
"No trouble at all, Mr. Frumble!" Mr.Fixit replies.
"I can do that in a jiffy."
"Oh, thank you, Mr. Fixit," Mr. Frumble says.

A moment later, Mr. Fixit reappears pushing
Mr. Frumble's pickle car outside.
"Voilà!" he says proudly...

..."Your skipickledoo!"

"Oh... my,"
gulps Mr. Frumble.

"And so that you can find your way, here is a compass to point you all the way to the North Pole," says Mr. Fixit.

"What are you going to do at the North Pole?" asks Mr. Fixit.
"I'm going to someone who needs my help," answers Mr. Frumble, "I'm going to be a Santa's helper!"

"Bon Voyage!" calls Mr. Fixit. "Don't forget to be home for Christmas! It's the day after tomorrow!"

SPROING!

SPROING!

SPROING!

SPROING!

Look out, everybody!
Here comes Mr. Frumble!

Mr. Frumble rides through rain.

He rides through fog.

He rides through snow.

He rides over tall mountains.

He rides down steep slopes!

... WOOPS!...

Mr. Frumble rides until the skipickledoo...

UMPF!

... can be ridden no more!

Santa's New Helper

"Dear me!" says Mr. Frumble. "Poor skipickledoo will need some repairs if I'm ever going to get to the North Pole! Lucky for me, that looks like a garage up ahead! I'm sure they can help me!"

Mr. Frumble walks in the door.
"Fill her up, please?" he calls. "Check the oil and water! Clean the windshield, please!...
Um... is anybody here?"

Rip!

WOAH!

BOOM!

Suddenly, Mr. Frumble slips on a puddle of water.

"Ho! Ho! Ho! And who are you?" asks a great big fellow in red trousers. Mr. Frumble explains that he needs his skipickledoo repaired so that he can get to the North Pole.

"Ho, ho, but you ARE at the North Pole! I'm Santa Bear and these are all my helpers."

Welcome!

"I'm afraid we're too busy making toys for all the good girls and boys, to repair your skipickledoo today," says Santa.

"Christmas is just two days away..." says Santa, pointing to the calendar on the wall.

"No... wait!" he cries.
"Ho, ho... Oh NO!
It's already December 24th!
It's Christmas Eve!"

"Helpers!" shouts Santa.
"Hurry! I have to go!"

"Get the sleigh ready and
bring the presents!"

"But we haven't finished yet!" squeak his helpers.

"Goodbye, helpers!" Santa calls, climbing the stairs to his sleigh.

Don't forget your hat, Santa!

Santa climbs into his big red sleigh.
"Are you ready, deers?" he asks.

He shakes the reins...

... and away he soars!

Mr. Frumble holds a calendar page in
his hands. "Um... I think this
came off when I came in," he says.

"Oh, no!" squeak the helpers. "Santa
has made a mistake! It isn't the night
before Christmas... it's the night
BEFORE the night before Christmas!"

The Night Before the Night Before Christmas

Santa flies over Busytown.
"That's odd," Santa says, "there are no Christmas lights on this year!"

Santa lands on the first rooftop, and disappears
down the chimney with his big bag of presents.
The bag is big but very light.

"Humpf!" says Santa, "this family has forgotten to decorate their Christmas tree!"

Santa continues to make his rounds through Busytown. "This is a very strange Christmas," thinks Santa. "Huckle, Sally and Lowly haven't hung up their stockings on the fireplace!"

"Hilda hasn't left a cup of cocoa and a plate of cookies, like she does every night before Christmas!"

"Sergeant Murphy hasn't even unpacked the Christmas tree!"

Finally, Santa Bear arrives at Mr. Frumble's house.
He slides with his bag down Mr. Frumble's chimney, but
Mr. Frumble's fireplace has become a locked broom closet!
Santa's sack has become stuck above him.

"Ho, ho," says Santa. "What do I do now?"

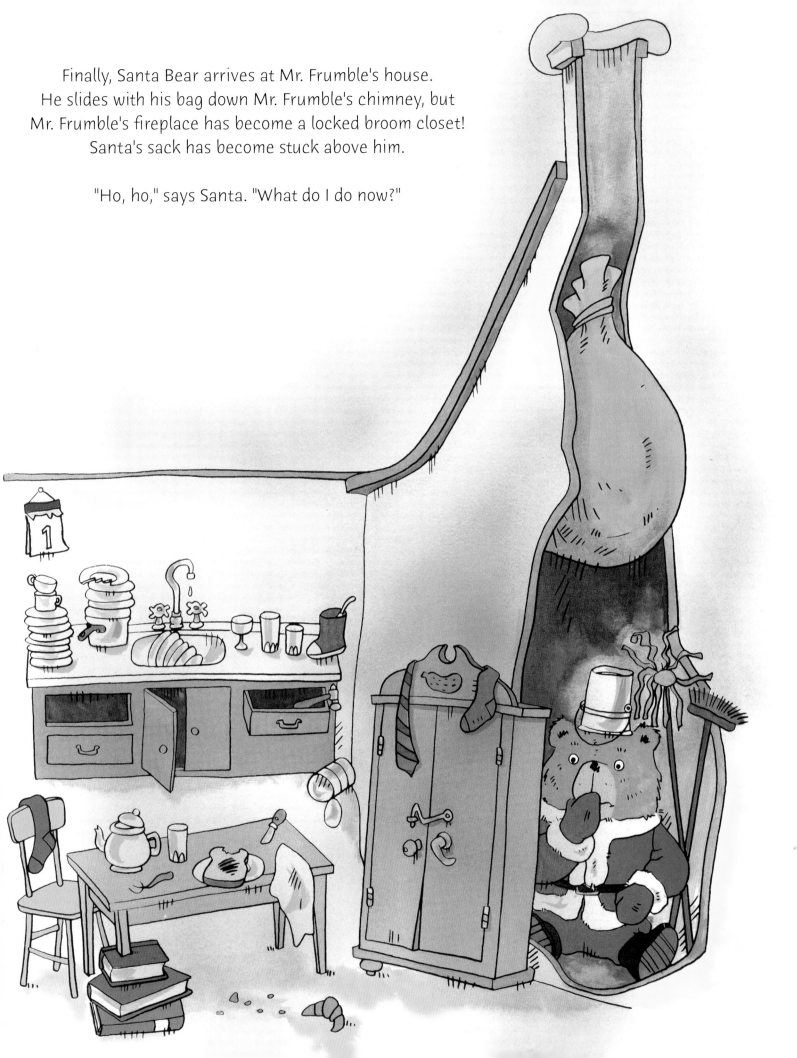

Santa Frumble

"What do we do now?" asks Mr. Frumble.
"We have to help Santa!" say Santa's helpers.

"Someone has to take Santa's place and deliver
the toys to all the good boys and girls for
Christmas!" says a Santa's helper

"But who will take Santa's place?" asks Mr. Frumble.
"YOU will!" answer all the Santa's helpers.

"ME? Santa?"

Meanwhile, the good boys and girls of
Busytown can't understand why they
all received presents before Christmas
Eve, and why all the boxes are empty!

"There must be a mistake!" says Lowly.

Santa's helpers work busily all day to finish
the toys they couldn't give to Santa Bear.
They repair Mr. Frumble's skipickledoo.

Mr. Frumble helps the
helpers fill the toy sack.

"How will we get to
Busytown?" Mr. Frumble asks.
"We will pull you!"
say Santa's helpers.

"But we don't know where Busytown is!" says a Santa's helper.
"Ah! But my hat does!" replies Mr. Frumble. "Hat always finds his way home!"
Mr. Frumble takes off his hat, and tosses it in the air.

Off flies the hat.
Off flies Santa Frumble and his busy helpers!

Good luck, Santa Frumble!

Tonight is the night before Christmas!

All of Busytown is decorated with colourful Christmas lights!

Santa Frumble lands at the Cat family house.

SWISH!

He climbs off his skipickledoo.

"Um... who goes down the chimney?" Santa Frumble asks the helpers. "YOU do!" they all reply.

Santa Frumble climbs down the
Cat family chimney.

BOOM!

Shhh! Santa Frumble! You don't
want to wake up the children!

Santa Frumble fills the
stockings that Huckle, Sally and Lowly
have hung on the fireplace.

Then he sits to sip some hot cocoa and eat
cookies the children have left for Santa Bear.

Santa Frumble gets up but trips in the dark. Woops! There goes the tree!

CRASH!

Shhh, Santa Frumble!

"Did you hear that?" says Sally excitedly. "I'll bet that was Santa!"

"Shhh!" whispers Huckle. "Go back to sleep, Sally... If Santa knows you're awake, he won't leave you a present."

Santa Frumble hurries on his way.

Santa Frumble visits Hilda Hippo's house.

He visits Sergeant Murphy's house.

And after he has visited every other house in Busytown, Santa Frumble arrives at his *own* house.

Santa Frumble looks
down his chimney.

Santa Frumble decides to enter his house through the front door.
What a clever Santa you are, Mr. Frumble!

He opens the broom closet.
"My hat!" he says.
"Our Santa!" say all the
Santa's helpers.

"What are you doing here?" Santa Bear asks Mr. Frumble.
"There was a big mistake at the North Pole," says Mr. Frumble.
"You left on the night before the night before
Christmas!" say Santa's helpers.

Thank goodness Santa Frumble was there to bring all the presents for good boys and girls on the night before Christmas!

Santa Bear thanks Santa Frumble, and rides back to the North Pole on his empty toy sack.

There is nothing left in Santa's sack, so Santa Bear leaves
Mr. Frumble the best present he can think of!

Wow! How about that!